Nelson the Blue Whale & Other Tales

by Laura Jaworski

Illustrated by Jerry Meyer

Nelson the Blue Whale

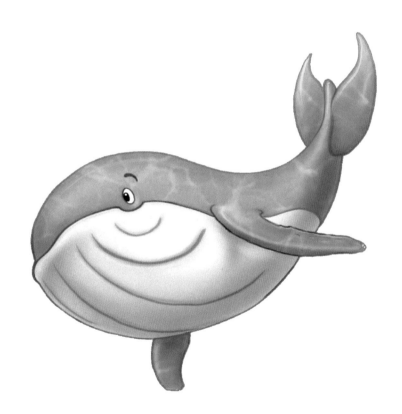

Nelson the blue whale is a very big whale.
He is the biggest whale there is!

Nelson's best friend is Nib, and he is a very tiny shrimp. So tiny, in fact, that Nelson has a hard time seeing him.

Can you see Nib?

Nelson and Nib do everything together.

They play together. They take naps together. They race together. And, when Nelson spurts water out of his blowhole, Nib rides to the very top of the waterspout.

Wheeee!

It is Nelson's birthday tomorrow, and his friends have planned a very special party.

The polar bears are bringing snow cones.

The seals are bringing coral confetti.

The walruses are bringing seaweed juice.

And, the penguins have helped Nib make a very special birthday present.

Nelson's birthday has finally arrived, and he is ready to open his present.

Can you see what Nib and the penguins have made for Nelson?

Why, they have made a pair of ice glasses!
Now Nelson can see Nib wherever they go!

Happy Birthday, Nelson!

Turtle Ball

Ugui the turtle loves to play games with his friends.

The turtles play tag. The turtles play hopscotch. The turtles play hide-and-seek. But, turtle ball is their very favorite game.

Ugui and his friends gather on top of a mountain every day to play turtle ball.

The turtles use their heads to bounce the ball back and forth.

Let's watch them play!

Uh oh! Ugui accidentally knocked the turtle ball off the mountain.

Down, down, down it goes!

How can the turtles play their game without a ball?

The turtles try to use a cake.

Will that work?

The turtles try to use a sandwich.

Will that work?

Ugui has an idea!

He has found the perfect ball!

Wheeeee!

Lola the Pink Elephant

Lola the pink elephant is very shy.

She is so shy, in fact, that she has not spoken to any of the other animals!

Lola is hiding behind a tree. She is hoping that no one can see her.

Can you see Lola?

The animals want to play with Lola!

The monkeys tell funny jokes, but Lola is too shy to come out.

The giraffes sing songs, but Lola is too shy to come out.

The lions play games, but Lola is too shy to come out.

Can you think of a way to help Lola come out from behind that tree?

Rhino has an idea!

We'll have a tea party on your side of the tree, Lola!

The End
(Until next time.)

For more books and fun visit
www.laurajaworski.com

Visit the illustrator at
gjmeyer.wix.com/portfolio

Made in the USA
Middletown, DE
13 December 2020